before

For Jem Angel Zehetner Love - H
For Hollie - J.P.

OXFORD
UNIVERSITY PRESS

Great Clarendon Street, Oxford OX2 6DP

Oxford University Press is a department of the University of Oxford.
It furthers the University's objective of excellence in research, scholarship,
and education by publishing worldwide in

Oxford   New York

Auckland Bangkok Buenos Aires Cape Town Chennai Dar es Salaam Delhi Hong Kong
Istanbul Karachi Kolkata Kuala Lumpur Madrid Melbourne Mexico City Mumbai Nairobi São Paulo
Shanghai Taipei Tokyo Toronto

Oxford is a registered trade mark of Oxford University Press in the UK and in certain other countries

Text © Hiawyn Oram 2003
Illustrations © Joanne Partis 2003

The moral rights of the author and artist have been asserted

Database right Oxford University Press (maker)

First published 2003

British Library Cataloguing in Publication Data available

ISBN 0-19-279095-1 (hardback)   ISBN 0-19-272550-5 (paperback)

3 5 7 9 10 8 6 4 2

Typeset in Maiandra

Printed in Singapore

The Good Mood Hunt

Hiawyn Oram

Joanne Partis

OXFORD

UNIVERSITY PRESS

Hannah woke happy.

Her eyes were shining. Her face was shining.
Her laugh was so catching everyone caught it...

even the dog...

even the cat...

even the canary!

And then she remembered
she had nothing to show
in Show and Tell...

and WHOA...

...suddenly she was all pouting and crumply.

'Oh no! Where's that good mood gone?'
cried her mother.

'I don't know,' Hannah pouted. 'It just WENT!'

'Well, it must be somewhere,' said her father.
'Better go and look for it!'

So Hannah went on the hunt for her good mood.

She looked in the
cupboard under the stairs
and the pockets of all the coats.

She found

lost gloves,

lost fluff,

lost money,

lost toffees...

...but no good mood,
not anywhere there.

'G'moooood!'

she called,
and went to look
in the dog's basket.

So she went to look under the bed.

She found

missing dinosaurs,
missing socks,
missing links,
missing library books...

...but no good mood,

not anywhere THERE!

'Found it?' called her brother.

'Not yet!' said Hannah. 'Could you help?'

'Sorry!' said her brother. 'Got to get to school.'
So Hannah went on with the hunt by herself.
'Good mood!' she called.

'G'moooo...ood!'

...and went to look in the garden shed.

She found

working
webs,

bursting-up
bulbs,

So into its emptiness
she carefully put

one *sleeping* centipede,

two missing dinosaurs,

three
old bones,

four lost toffees,

and a kiss for good luck...

...and she was off, pulling on her coat and hat,

begging to be taken to school,

but please hurry up this minute.

'I see you found your
good mood!' laughed her mother as
they hopped, skipped, and ran all the way.

'Oh, yes!' said Hannah.
'It's right in this box!'

And when she opened the box for Show and Tell there it was!

Forgotten party toffees!

Bones buried like pirate treasure, maybe for years and years!

Dinosaurs we thought had gone for ever ...

... and a sleeping centipede ... ah ... suddenly waking up!

Hannah laughed with a laugh so catching everyone caught it!

And after that, whenever there were bad mooders in class,

guess what the teacher sent them on?

One of Hannah's
Good Mood
Hunts!

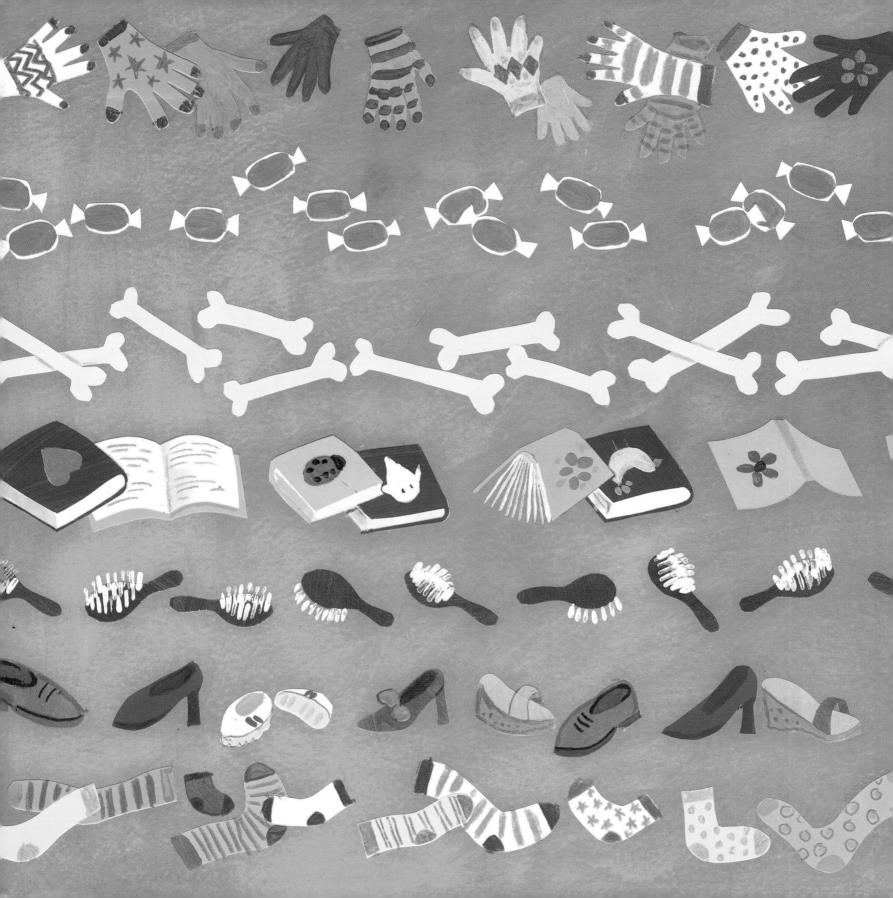